The Little Mermaid

Also includes

The True-Hearted Tin Soldier

Hans Christian Andersen

Translated by Misha Hoekstra   Illustrated by Helen Crawford-White

PUSHKIN CHILDREN'S BOOKS

Pushkin Press
71–75 Shelton Street
London WC2H 9JQ

English translation of "The Little Mermaid" and "The True-Hearted
Tin Soldier" © 2019 Misha Hoekstra

"The Little Mermaid" was originally published in Danish in 1837 as
"Den Lille Havfrue" in *Eventyr, Fortalte for Børn: Første Samling*

"The True-Hearted Tin Soldier" was originally published in Danish
in 1838 as "Den Standhaftige Tinsoldat" in *Eventyr, Fortalte for Børn:
Ny Samling*

Illustrations © Helen Crawford-White 2019

First published by Pushkin Press in 2019

9 8 7 6 5 4 3 2 1

ISBN 13: 978-1-78269-249-2

Designed and typeset by Tetragon, London

Printed and bound by in Great Britain by TJ International, Padstow,
Cornwall on Munken Premium Pure 120gsm

www.pushkinpress.com

The Little Mermaid

AR OUT AT SEA, the water is as blue as cornflower petals and as clear as the purest glass. Yet it's very deep—deeper than the reach of any anchor rope. You'd have to stack a lot of steeples on top of each other to reach from the bottom to the surface. And down at the bottom is where the sea folk live.

Now, you mustn't think that the sea floor is only bare white sand—no, because the most marvellous trees and plants grow there. Their leaves and stems are so flexible, the smallest movement of water makes them sway as if they were dancing. All the fish, big and small, flit through their branches, just like birds in the air up here. In the deepest spot of all stands the palace of the Sea King. Its walls are coral and its high pointed windows the clearest amber, while the roof is made of clamshells that open and close with the current. It looks magnificent, because in each shell there are glistening pearls, and any one of them would be the pride of a queen's crown.

The Sea King had been widowed for many years, and his old mother ran the royal household. She was a wise mermaid, though proud of her high rank; so she paraded about with twelve oysters on her tail, while the other mermaids at court could only have six. But she was admirable in all other things, especially her affection for the young sea princesses—her granddaughters. There were six of these lovely princesses, but the youngest was the most beautiful of all. Her skin glowed like a rose petal and her eyes were as blue as the deepest sea. And just like her sisters, she had no feet, for her body ended in a fish's tail.

All day long they played in the great palace halls, where living flowers grew from the walls. When they threw open the tall amber windows, the fish would swim inside, just as swallows fly through our windows when we open them. But these fish swam right over to the little princesses, ate from their hands and let themselves be petted.

Outside the palace lay a large garden with trees that were fiery red and navy blue. The fruit shone like gold and the flowers looked like burning flames, their stems and leaves forever flickering. The ground was the finest sand, but it was the blue colour of sulphur when it burns. Everything was bathed in a wonderful azure glow, so that you might imagine you were high in the air, gazing only at the sky above and below you, rather than at the ocean floor. When the sea was calm, you could glimpse the crimson flower that all the light seemed to be streaming from—the sun.

Each princess had her own little garden plot where she could dig and plant just as she wished. One made her flowerbed in the shape of a whale, another preferred a small mermaid, but the youngest made hers perfectly round like the sun, and only planted flowers that glowed with the same red colour. She was a strange child, quiet and thoughtful. While the other sisters decorated their gardens with the many marvellous things they had taken from shipwrecks, hers had only one thing besides its rosy red, sunlike flowers. This was a beautiful marble statue, a handsome boy carved from bright white stone, which had sunk with a ship to the bottom of the sea. Next to this statue she planted a red weeping willow that grew wild and lush. Its long, slender branches hung down over the boy and stretched towards the blue sandy seabed, where they cast violet shadows that were always moving, just like the branches. It looked as if the leaves and roots were playing a kissing game.

Her greatest delight was to hear stories about the human world above, and the old grandmother had to tell her and her sisters everything she knew about ships and towns, people and animals. It amazed the little Princess that up on land the flowers had scents, as they didn't smell of anything at the bottom of the ocean; and that the forests were green, and the fish in the branches could sing so loudly and lovely, it was pure pleasure. "Fish" was what their grandmother called songbirds, for otherwise the princesses couldn't understand her—because they had never seen a bird.

"The day you turn fifteen," their grandmother told them, "you'll be allowed to go up into the open air, sit on the rocks in the moonlight and watch the great ships sail past. You'll see towns and forests too!"

Later that year, the first of the sisters would be fifteen, but the others—well, there was a year between each of their ages. That meant the youngest had five long years to wait before she could swim up from the bottom of the ocean and glimpse the things that you and I see every day. But each sister promised to tell the others the best things she saw and heard on her first day above water, because their grandmother didn't tell them nearly enough. And there was so much they wanted to know.

No one was filled with more longing than the youngest, who was precisely the one who had to wait the longest and was so quiet and thoughtful. Many nights, she lingered by her open window and looked up through the dark blue water, where the fish were flapping their fins and tails. She could see the moon and stars shining—quite faintly to be sure, yet through the water they seemed much larger than to our eyes. Once in a while, something like a big black cloud would glide overhead and blot them out, and then she knew it was either a whale swimming above her, or a ship sailing past, filled with people. They certainly weren't thinking that a sweet little mermaid might be far beneath them, stretching her white hands up towards the keel.

Then the oldest princess turned fifteen and ventured up above the surface of the sea.

When she returned, she had a hundred things to tell. But the loveliest thing of all, she said, was lying in the moonlight on a sandbar in the calm sea and looking up at the big town near the shore, where the lights twinkled like a hundred stars; listening to the music, and the clatter and racket of wagons and people; seeing all the steeples and spires; and hearing how the bells pealed. Since she couldn't go up on land, those were things the oldest sister yearned for most of all.

Oh, how intently the youngest sister listened! And later that evening, when she was at her open window, gazing up through the dark blue water, she imagined the great town with all its noise and bustle, and she thought she could hear the church bells ringing down to her.

The next year, the second sister was allowed to swim up through the water and go wherever she wished. She surfaced just as the sun was setting, and that was the sight she found prettiest. The entire sky was golden, she said, and the clouds. . . Well, she could hardly describe their beauty! Red and violet, they had sailed overhead. But flying much faster than the clouds was something like a long white veil—a flock of wild swans that flew across the water to where the sun perched on the edge. She swam towards the sun until it sank, and then the rosy glow faded from the face of the sea and the clouds.

The year after that, the third sister made the journey to the top, and since she was the most daring of them all, she swam up a broad river that flowed out into the sea. She saw pretty green hills with grapevines, and castles and farms peeping through magnificent forests. She listened to how all the birds sang, and the sun blazed so hot that she kept ducking underwater to cool her burning face. At a bend in the river she came upon an entire group of human children. They ran about quite naked, splashing in the water. She wanted to play, but they ran away frightened, and then a small black animal ran down to the water. It was a dog, but she'd never seen a dog before, and it barked so fiercely that she got scared and hurried back to the open ocean. But never would she forget the splendid forests, the green hills or the charming children who could swim—even without tails.

The fourth sister was not so bold, and so she stayed out in the middle of the wild ocean. She told the others that it was definitely the best place to be because she could see for miles around, and the sky arched overhead like an immense glass bell. Ships far off in the distance bobbed like seagulls; playful dolphins turned somersaults; and huge whales spouted water through their blowholes, so that it looked as if a hundred fountains were spraying all around her.

A year later it was the fifth sister's turn. Her birthday was in winter, and so she saw things that none of the others had seen on their first day. The ocean appeared quite green, and all about her floated great icebergs. Each one resembled a pearl, she said, and yet they were much bigger in size than the church towers that people built. They had the most fantastic shapes and they glittered like diamonds. She had seated herself on one of the largest ones, and the sailing boats all kept their distance, their crews terrified, while she sat there and let her hair fly in the wind. Then, late in the evening, clouds covered the sky, lightning flashed and thunder cracked, and the black sea heaved the huge ice blocks high in the air, to be lit for an instant by blue lightning. The ships all lowered their sails in fear and horror, yet the fifth sister sat calmly on her floating iceberg and watched the blue bolts zigzag into the bright ocean.

The first time each sister had come up into the air, she'd been overjoyed at all the new and beautiful things she saw. But once she was allowed to go up there anytime she wished, it no longer seemed so special and she would pine for the others. And after a month had passed, she would say that the most beautiful place was down on the sea floor, and nothing was as pleasant as home.

Nevertheless, the five older sisters would often join arms in the evenings and swim to the surface in a row. They had lovely voices—lovelier than any human voices. And when a storm was brewing and they thought that ships might sink, they would swim in front of them and sing sweetly about how wonderful it was at the bottom of the sea, and how the sailors shouldn't be afraid to go down there. But the sailors couldn't understand their words; they thought it was the storm singing. Nor did they ever get to see the wonders of the deep, because when a ship sank, the sailors drowned, and the only way they could enter the palace of the Sea King was as dead men.

Every evening that the sisters swam up through the ocean, arm in arm, they would leave their younger sister behind, floating there all alone and gazing up after them. And each time it seemed as if she would cry. But a mermaid has no tears, and so she suffers all the more.

"Oh, how I wish I were fifteen!" she would lament. "I know that I'll learn to love the upper world—and all the people who live there and build so many things!"

Then finally her birthday came, and at last she was fifteen.

"Well, at least you'll be off my hands now," said her grandmother, the old Queen. "Come on, let's dress you up, just like your sisters!" She placed a wreath of white lilies on the little mermaid's head, and each petal was made from half a pearl. Then she ordered eight oysters to clamp themselves tightly to her granddaughter's tail, to show her high rank.

"Ouch! That hurts!" the little mermaid said.

"Naturally," the old mermaid replied. "One must suffer to keep up appearances."

Oh, how she wanted to take off the heavy wreath and shake off all that finery! The red flowers in her garden would have suited her much better, but she didn't dare undo her grandmother's work. "Goodbye," the little mermaid said—and then she rose up through the water, as light and bright as a bubble.

The sun had just gone down when her head peeped above the surface. All the clouds gleamed like roses and gold, and the evening star shone brilliant and fine in the middle of a pink sky. The air was fresh and mild, the sea completely calm. A large ship with three masts lay upon the water with just a single sail unfurled, for there was hardly a breath of a breeze. Sailors perched on the spars

and rigging. There was music and song, and as the evening grew dark, the crew lit a hundred lanterns of every colour; it looked like the flags of all nations were fluttering in the breeze.

The little mermaid swam up to a porthole, and each time a swell lifted her in the air she caught a glimpse of finely dressed people through the glass. The handsomest of them all was a young prince with large jet-black eyes. He wasn't much more than sixteen—in fact, it was his birthday too, and that's why there was so much pomp and hullaballoo. Then the sailors began to dance on deck and, when the Prince stepped out, scores of rockets shot through the air and the ship lit up as bright as day, which frightened the little mermaid and made her dive underwater. But she quickly poked her head up again, and it seemed as if all the stars of heaven were tumbling down around her. Never had she seen such fireworks! Big suns spun round, splendid fire-fish swooped down out of nowhere, and all of it was reflected in the calm, clear sea. It made everything so brilliant on board that she could see every little rope, to say nothing of the people. My, how handsome the young Prince looked! He shook everyone's hand, laughing and smiling as music rang out in the gorgeous night.

It grew late, but the little mermaid couldn't tear her eyes from the ship and the fine Prince. After a time, the coloured lanterns were blown out and no more rockets split the air; no more cannons boomed. Yet the deeps of the ocean hummed and thrummed around her as she floated there, bobbing up and down so she could peer through the porthole. Then the ship began to move and it picked up speed as sail after sail was unfurled and filled with wind. Now the waves grew higher, great clouds gathered and lightning flashed in the distance. Oh, the weather was turning terrible! The sailors took down the sails, and the great ship plunged through the wild ocean. The water rose up like black mountains, trying to knock down the masts, and the ship slid down the great waves like a swan before climbing back up the towering crests.

The little mermaid still thought this was all great fun—but not the sailors. The ship creaked and cracked, its thick planks bulging from the mighty beating of the sea. Then the mainmast snapped in the middle like a matchstick and the ship pitched over on its side as water rushed into the hold. Now the little mermaid saw the danger they were in as she dodged spinning beams and timbers in the water. One moment everything would be black as coal and she couldn't see a thing, then lightning would strike and for an instant it would be so bright, she could recognize each person on deck, tumbling every which way. She searched and sought for the Prince—and then, just as the ship was breaking up, she saw him plummet into the deep sea.

The little mermaid rejoiced, for now he was coming down to join her! But then she remembered that people cannot live underwater, and that he couldn't enter her father's palace except as a dead man. *Don't die,* she thought, *you mustn't!* And she swam in among the pitching planks and timbers, completely forgetting that they could crush her, diving deep beneath the flotsam and coming up high among the waves till at last she reached the young Prince. He could barely swim another stroke, his arms and legs faltering in the heaving sea, and his beautiful eyes closed. He would have drowned if the little mermaid hadn't reached him, but now she held his head above the water and let the storm drive the two of them wherever the waves wished.

By early morning the bad weather had passed. Not a splinter remained of the ship. The sun rose from the ocean, so red and bright that it seemed to restore the Prince's cheeks to life, yet his eyes stayed shut. The mermaid stroked the wet hair back from his fine high forehead and kissed it. He looked like the marble statue in her little garden, she thought, and she kissed him again. *If only he might live.*

Now she could see the mainland in front of them, with its high blue mountains where the white snow shone like sleeping swans. Gorgeous green forests stretched along the coast, and before them rose a church or a convent, she really didn't know, but a building in any case. Lemon and orange trees grew in the courtyard, and tall palm trees stood before the gates. The sea here formed a small bay, glassy but very deep. She swam with the handsome Prince up to the base of a cliff and laid him down on the fine white sand at its foot, making sure his head was resting in the warm sunshine.

The bells in the large white building began to peal, and a throng of young girls filtered through the courtyard. The little mermaid swam back behind some high rocks that stuck up from the water. There she covered her hair and upper body with foam so that no one would notice her small face peering out, watching to see who might find the poor Prince.

It didn't take long. The girl who discovered him seemed quite frightened, but only for a moment. Then she got more people, and the mermaid saw the Prince wake up. He smiled at all the people around him, but not at the little mermaid; he didn't even know she was there. She felt devastated. And when they led him into the big building she dived deep into the water, full of sorrow, and found her way back to her father's palace.

The little mermaid had always been quiet and thoughtful; now she was even more so. Her sisters asked her what she'd seen during her first time above water, but she wouldn't tell them anything.

Often in the morning and evening she would swim up to where she'd left the Prince. She watched how the fruit in the garden ripened; she watched how it was plucked. She watched how the snow melted on the high mountains. But she never saw the Prince, and so she would turn home sadder than ever. Her only comfort was to sit in her little garden and fling her arms around the handsome marble statue that looked so much like the Prince. But she didn't tend her flowers, and they grew wild—spreading out across the paths, braiding their long stems and leaves into the branches of the trees, till her garden became quite dark.

In the end the little mermaid couldn't bear it any longer and told one of her sisters, and straight away all her other sisters knew. But no one else did—except for a couple of the other mermaids, who only told their closest friends. And one of them happened to know who the Prince was; she had seen the fancy ship too, and she told them where he came from and where his kingdom lay.

"Come, little sister!" the other princesses called. And with their arms draped around each other's shoulders, the six of them rose from the ocean in a long row in front of the Prince's castle.

It was built of gleaming, pale yellow stone, with a great marble staircase that ran right down to the sea. Majestic gilt domes swelled on the roofline, and marble statues peeped from among the columns circling the castle and appeared to be alive. Through the tall windows the little mermaid glimpsed the most splendid halls, where expensive silk curtains hung and the walls were decorated with large paintings that must have been a pleasure to gaze upon. An enormous fountain burbled in the middle of the biggest hall, and jets of water stretched high towards the glass dome, through which the sun streamed onto the water and the lovely plants growing in the large pool.

Now the little mermaid knew where the Prince lived, and she spent many nights in the sea offshore. She went much closer to land than any of her sisters dared—yes, she even swam up the narrow canal beneath the grand marble balcony. Here, in the long shadow that it cast onto the water, she would study the young Prince, who thought he was all by himself in the bright moonlight.

Often she watched him sailing in his magnificent ship in the evenings, with music playing and flags aflutter. She'd peek at him from among the green reeds, and the wind would catch the long silver-white veil she wore. If anyone saw it, they simply thought it was a swan, lifting its wings.

On some nights, the fishermen would light lanterns on their boats to catch eels. She would paddle close and listen as they told each other tales of the young Prince's goodness, and it made her happy to think that she'd saved his life when he almost died in the waves. And she remembered how steadily he had rested on her breast, how passionately she had kissed him. Yet he knew nothing of what had happened—no, he couldn't even dream about her.

The little mermaid grew fonder and fonder of human beings, and she wished more and more that she could walk up among them. Their world seemed so much larger than hers, for they could fly across the sea in ships and climb the mountains till they were higher than the clouds, while the lands they owned, with their fields and forests, stretched farther than her eyes could see. There was so much she longed to know! Yet her sisters couldn't answer all her questions, and so she asked her grandmother. The old mermaid knew a lot about the upper world, as she quite rightly called the lands above the sea.

"If they don't drown, can human beings live forever?" the little mermaid asked her. "Or do they have to die, like we do down here in the sea?"

"Yes, they must die too," her grandmother said. "And their lifetime is even shorter than ours. We can live to be three hundred years old—though when *we* stop living, we turn into foam on the water. And we have no graves here, down among those we love. We don't have immortal souls; there's no more life for us once we die. A mermaid is just like a green reed—once it's been cut down, it will never grow new leaves! But a human being has a soul that lives forever. This soul keeps living after the human body turns into soil; it rises up through the clear air, up to all the twinkling stars! Just as we can rise to the top of the ocean to look at the lands of people, so people can rise to amazing unknown places that we will never get to see."

"Why don't *we* have an immortal soul?" asked the little mermaid, disappointed. "I'd gladly give up my three hundred years if I could just live for a single day as a human—and then become part of that heavenly world!"

"Don't say such things!" the old mermaid warned. "We're much happier and better off than the people up there."

"But then I'm going to die and just turn into foam floating on the ocean! I won't hear the music of the waves any more, or see all the fine flowers and the red sun! Isn't there anything at all I can do to get an immortal soul?"

"No!" her grandmother insisted. "Except. . . except if a human being loved you so much that you meant more to him than his mother and father, if he would do anything for you and let a minister place his right hand in yours, and if you both promised to be true to each other, now and forever. Then his soul would flow into your body, and you would know lasting human happiness. He would give you a soul—and keep his too.

"But that'll never happen!" the old mermaid continued. "The one thing that we admire so much here in the sea—our fishtail—seems hideous to people on land. Human beings have no sense. They think that to be beautiful, you need the two clumsy stumps they call legs!"

The little mermaid sighed, and looked sadly at her fishtail.

"Let's enjoy ourselves," her grandmother said. "Let's leap and dance for the three hundred years we have. That's plenty of time—and when we die, we can rest, and that'll feel more pleasant then. Meanwhile, tonight we're holding a court ball!"

Indeed, the mermaid ball was finer than anything you'll ever see on land. The walls and ceiling of the ballroom were made of thick glass, and hundreds of gigantic clamshells, rosy red and grassy green, stood in lines on both sides, while a burning blue fire lit up the sea around the ballroom. Innumerable fish, big and small, could be seen swimming towards the glass walls; some had scales of glowing purple, on others the scales were silver and gold. A broad current flowed through the ballroom, where mermen and mermaids danced to their own wonderful songs. Never will you hear such voices up here! And the little mermaid's singing was the loveliest of all, and everyone clapped. For a moment her heart was glad, because she knew she had the most beautiful voice anywhere, on land or in the sea.

But soon she started thinking about the upper world. She couldn't forget the handsome Prince, or her sorrow over not having what he did—an immortal soul. So she slipped out of her father's palace, and while everything inside was laughter and song, she sat in her little garden, mournful and alone. Then she heard the sound of a horn coming down through the water, and she thought to herself, *He's probably sailing above me right now—the one person who means more to me than father or mother, the one person I'm devoted to and in whose hand I want to place my life's happiness. I'd risk everything to win him, and a soul! Maybe the Sea Witch can give me advice and help, even though she's always scared me. Yes—while my sisters are dancing in our father's palace, I'll visit the Sea Witch.*

The little mermaid swam from her garden towards the seething whirlpools. Somewhere behind them lived the witch. The little mermaid had never gone that way before, for no flowers grew there, not even seaweed. There was only bare grey sea floor until she got to the whirlpools, where the water whooshed around like roaring mill wheels and brought everything it caught down into the deeps. She had to swim through the middle of the deadly whirlpools to reach the region of the sea witch, and then the only way was across the hot bubbling swamp that the witch called her peat bog. Beyond the swamp was a strange jungle, with the witch's house at the centre. The trees and bushes here were all polyps, half animal and half plant; they looked like hundred-headed snakes growing from the ground. Their branches were long slimy arms with flexible fingers like worms, squirming joint by joint from root to tip. Whenever the polyps could grab hold of something, they coiled themselves tightly around it and never let go.

The little mermaid was terrified as she floated there in front of them, her heart pounding with fear, and she almost turned around. But then she thought of the Prince, and a human soul, and she took courage. She tied her flowing hair around her head, so that the polyps couldn't grab it, crossed both hands over her breast and flew through the water the way only a fish can, scooting in between all the monstrous polyps that stretched out their waving tentacles to catch her. She saw that wherever a polyp had captured something, a hundred small tentacles were holding it fast like strong bands of iron. Humans who had drowned at

sea and sunk to the bottom were only white skeletons now, peeping forth from the polyps' arms. She could see ships' rudders and sea chests that had fallen into their clutches, the bones of land animals and—scariest of all—a small mermaid they'd caught and strangled.

Now she came to a large slimy clearing in the jungle where big fat sea snakes squirmed around and showed their vile yellowish bellies. In the middle of the clearing, a house had been built from the white bones of shipwrecked sailors. And there sat the Sea Witch, letting a toad eat from her mouth, just the way we might let a canary peck at a sugar lump between our teeth. "My little chickens!" she called out to the nasty fat sea snakes, and they wriggled up onto her big spongy breast.

"I know what you want," cried the Sea Witch, "and it's a stupid thing to ask! Yet I will let you have your way, my darling Princess, for I know it'll bring you misfortune. You'd like to get rid of your fishtail, and instead you want two stumps to walk with, like the humans—just so the young Prince might fall in love with you, and then you can win him and an immortal soul!"

The witch's laughter was so loud and evil that the toad and the sea snakes fell to the ground, where they continued to twitch and writhe. "You've come at just the right time," said the witch. "Tomorrow, when the sun comes up, I wouldn't be able to help you for another year. But I'll make you a potion, and before the sun rises, you must swim to land, sit on the shore and drink it. It'll split your tail in two, and the two pieces will shrivel into what humans call pretty legs. But it will hurt! It'll feel like a sharp sword has sliced right through you. Then everyone who catches sight of you will say that you're the loveliest person they've ever seen. You'll keep your swaying way of moving, and no dancer will be able to glide like you—but with every step you take, it'll feel like you're stepping on a sharp knife that'll make you bleed. Do you want me to help you suffer all of this?"

"Yes!" said the little mermaid with a trembling voice, thinking of the Prince and the undying soul that would be hers.

"But remember," said the witch, "once you have a human shape, you can never be a mermaid again! Never can you swim down through the water to your sisters or to your father's palace. And if you *don't* win the Prince's love—if he *doesn't* forget father and mother, promise himself to you and let the minister place your hands together as husband and wife—then you'll never get a soul! If he marries someone else instead, your heart will burst the very next time the sun rises, and you'll turn into sea foam."

"I'll do it!" cried the little mermaid, and she turned as pale as a corpse.

"Ah, but you must pay me too," said the witch. "And it's no small thing I ask! You have the most beautiful voice of anyone at the bottom of the sea—and you probably think you can use it to enchant him. But you must give that voice to me! The very best thing you have—that's the price of this precious potion. For I must put my own blood into it, to make the potion as sharp as a double-edged sword."

"But once you take my voice, what will I have left?"

"You'll have your lovely form, the floating way you move, and your expressive eyes," the witch said. "With these three things, surely you can charm a human heart? Ha, have you lost your courage? Stick out your little tongue! I'll cut it off as payment—and then you'll get your potion."

"Do it!" said the little mermaid.

The Sea Witch set her cauldron on the fire to boil the magic potion. She tied the sea snakes in a knot and used them to scour out the cauldron. "Cleanliness is a virtue!" she said. Then she cut herself on the breast and let her black blood drip into the cauldron, and the steam formed the eeriest shapes—shapes that would terrify anyone. The witch kept adding new things to the cauldron, and it bubbled away, like the tears in a crocodile's eyes. Finally the potion was ready—and it looked just like pure water.

"Here you go!" said the witch, and then she sliced off the little mermaid's tongue. Now she was mute, unable to sing or speak.

"When the polyps try to grab you on your way back through the jungle," the witch said, "just splash a single drop of the potion on them. Then their arms and fingers will burst into smithereens."

But that wasn't necessary. When the polyps saw the potion in the little mermaid's hand, glittering like a star, they drew back in fear. And so she passed quickly through the jungle, the swamp and the roaring whirlpools.

Now she could see her father's palace. The flames in the great ballroom had all been snuffed out. She supposed everyone was asleep inside, but she didn't dare to try to find them, because now she was mute and leaving them forever. She felt as if her heart would break in pieces from sorrow. She sneaked into the garden and took one blossom from each of her sisters' flowerbeds, flung a thousand kisses towards the palace and swam up through the deep blue sea.

The sun hadn't risen yet when she reached the Prince's castle and crawled up its majestic marble steps; but the moon still shone wonderfully bright. The little mermaid drank down the burning bitter potion, and then her delicate body felt like it was being split by a double-edged sword. She fainted and lay there lifeless. When the first ray of the sun touched the ocean, she woke and felt a sizzling pain, but just in front of her stood the handsome young Prince, his coal-black eyes fixed upon her. She dropped her gaze and saw that her fishtail was gone; instead she had the prettiest legs a girl could wish for, slender and white. Since she had no clothes, she wrapped herself in her long flowing hair. The Prince asked her who she was and how she had got there. She gazed at him with gentleness in her dark blue eyes and yet sadness too, for of course she couldn't speak. Then he took her by the hand and led her into the castle. Just as the witch had said, with each step it felt like she was walking on sharp knives and needles, but she put up with it gladly. She glided up the stairs at his side as lightly as a bubble, and the Prince and everyone who saw her marvelled at the graceful, floating way she walked.

They gave her expensive clothes of silk and muslin to wear, and she was the prettiest in the castle. Yet she could not sing or speak. Lovely servant women in silk and gold came out and sang for the Prince and his royal parents. One servant sang more beautifully than the others, and the Prince clapped his hands and smiled at her. That saddened the little mermaid, for she knew she could have sung far better. *Oh*, she thought, *if only he knew that I gave away my voice forever just to be with him!*

Then the servants began a charming, gliding dance to magnificent music. The little mermaid raised her fine white arms, rose up on tiptoe and floated across the floor, dancing like no one had ever danced before. With each movement her loveliness became more and more apparent, while her eyes spoke to the depths of the heart, deeper than the servants singing. Everyone was enchanted—especially the Prince, who called her his little foundling—and she kept dancing, even though each time her foot touched the floor it felt like she was stepping on knife blades.

The Prince declared that she must stay with him always, and she was allowed to sleep outside his door on a velvet pillow. He let her sew herself men's clothing so that she could follow him on horseback. They rode through fragrant forests, where green branches slapped her shoulders and songbirds sang behind new leaves. She climbed the high mountains with the Prince, and though her fine feet bled so that everyone noticed, she laughed it off and followed him upwards, till they saw the clouds sailing beneath them like a flock of birds flying to far-off lands.

Back home in the Prince's castle, the little mermaid would walk out onto the broad marble steps at night while the others slept. The cold seawater cooled her burning feet as she stood there, and then she'd think about the sea folk who lived in the deeps.

One night her sisters appeared, arm in arm, singing mournfully as they swam through the water. She waved to them, and then they saw who she was. They told her how sad she'd made them. They visited every night after that, and once she even saw in the distance her old grandmother, who hadn't been above water in many years, and the Sea King with his crown upon his head. They stretched their arms towards her, but they didn't dare to come as close to shore as her sisters.

Day by day, the little mermaid became dearer and dearer to the Prince. He doted on her, the way you dote on a darling child. Yet it never occurred to him to make her his queen. And she *had* to become his wife! Otherwise she wouldn't gain an immortal soul, and when day dawned after his wedding, she would turn into foam.

When he took her in his arms and kissed her beautiful forehead, the little mermaid's eyes seemed to ask, *Don't you love me more than anyone else?*

"You are the dearest of them all," the Prince said, "because you have the truest heart and show the most devotion to me. Besides, you remind me of a girl I once saw but will probably never see again. I was on a ship that sank, and the waves carried me to land near a holy temple where some young women were serving. The youngest one found me on the shore and rescued me, but

I only saw her twice. She's the only person I could love in this world—though you do look like her and have almost replaced her image in my heart. Since she belongs to the temple, my good fortune has sent you to me instead—and never shall we be apart!"

Alas, thought the little mermaid, *he doesn't realize that I was the one who saved his life! I bore him across the ocean to the shore where that temple stands, then hid myself in foam and watched to see if anyone would come. And then I saw her—the beautiful girl he loves more than me!* The mermaid sighed deeply, since she could not cry. *That girl belongs to the holy temple, that's what he said. She'll never leave and go out into the world, and that means they'll never meet again. But I am at his side and see him every day—and I'll care for him, love him and sacrifice my life for him!*

Yet then people began to say that the Prince was to be married—to the neighbouring king's lovely daughter! That's why he's fitting out such a stately ship, they said. The Prince is making the journey just to see the kingdom, that's the official story—but the real reason he's taking so many people along is because he's going to see the King's daughter.

The little mermaid only shook her head and laughed. She knew the Prince's thoughts better than anyone. "I *have* to go!" he had told her. "I *have* to see this beautiful princess—my parents insist. But can they force me to bring her home as my bride? Never! I cannot love her! She can't possibly look like the beautiful girl in the temple, as you do. If I were ever going to choose a bride, I'd rather choose you, my silent foundling with the eloquent eyes!" And then he'd kissed her red lips, twirled her long hair around his fingers and placed his head by her heart, so that it dreamt of human happiness and an immortal soul.

"You certainly don't act afraid of the ocean, my silent girl!" said the Prince when they stood upon the stately ship that was bringing him to the neighbouring kingdom. And he explained all about storms and calms, about the curious fish in the deeps and all the things that divers had seen down there. The little mermaid smiled at his explanations. After all, she knew more about the bottom of the sea than anyone.

In the moon-bright night, while all the others slept except the first mate standing at the wheel, she sat by the ship's railing and stared down through the clear water. She imagined she could see her father's palace, and at the top of it her old grandmother, wearing her silver crown and staring up through the swift current towards the ship's keel. Just then, her sisters swam up to the surface and gazed mournfully at her, twisting their white hands. She waved to them, smiling; she wanted to tell them that everything was going well, that she was happy. But then the cabin boy approached and her sisters dived out of sight, and he thought the white flash he'd seen was just some foam on the sea.

The next morning, the ship sailed into the harbour of the neighbouring king's glorious city. All the church bells were ringing, trumpets sounded from high towers and soldiers stood to attention, their banners fluttering and bayonets glinting. Every day there was some new party, a ball or society gathering, one after the other, and yet the Princess did not appear. She lived far from the city, they said, in some holy temple where they were teaching her all the royal virtues. Then finally one day she arrived.

The little mermaid had been eager to see her beauty, and she had to admit that she'd never seen anyone more striking. The Princess's skin was so fine and fair, and beneath her long dark eyelashes smiled a pair of devoted black-blue eyes.

"It's you!" cried the Prince. "You rescued me when I lay like a corpse on the shore!" And he wrapped his arms around his blushing bride-to-be.

Then he turned to the little mermaid. "Oh, I am just too happy!" he told her. "The best thing that could happen to me, the one thing I never dared to hope for, has come true! And I'm sure that you share my joy, because you love me more than anyone does." The little mermaid kissed his hand and felt that her heart would burst. The dawn after his wedding would bring her death and turn her into foam on the sea.

The church bells were pealing and heralds rode through the streets to proclaim the news. Scented oils burned in silver lamps on every altar. The ministers swung their incense burners, and then bride and groom took each other by the hand and received the bishop's blessing. The little mermaid stood in silk and gold and held the train of the bride's dress. But her ears did not hear the festive music, and her eyes did not see the holy ceremony. She was thinking of her dying night, and of everything she'd lost in this world.

That very same evening, bride and groom went on board the Prince's ship. The cannons boomed, the flags waved, and in the middle of the ship a royal tent of gold and purple was raised and furnished with the finest cushions. The newlyweds were to sleep there that quiet, cool night. The sails swelled in the breeze and the ship glided effortlessly across the bright ocean.

When darkness fell, the coloured lanterns were lit and the sailors danced merrily upon the deck. The little mermaid couldn't help but think about the first time she rose from the sea and saw the same splendour and joy, and she threw herself into the whirling dance, gliding and twirling like a swallow being pursued. And everyone cheered in wonder, for never had she danced so fantastically. The dance cut her fine feet like knives, yet she didn't feel it; the real pain was in her heart. She knew that this was the last night she would see the young man for whom she'd left her home and family, for whom she'd given her beautiful voice and for whom she'd suffered torment every day. And she knew that he had no notion of what she'd sacrificed. It was the last night she was breathing the same air as he, seeing the same deep sea and starry sky. An eternal night without thought or dream was waiting for her—a mermaid who had no soul and could not earn one. And everything on the ship was joy and merriment until long past midnight. She laughed and danced with the shadow of death in her heart. Then the Prince kissed his darling bride, she played with his black hair, and the two of them walked arm in arm to rest in their magnificent tent.

It grew hushed and silent on board the ship. Only the first mate remained, standing by the wheel. The little mermaid rested her white arms upon the railing and looked to the east for the dawn. The first sunbeam, she knew, would kill her. Then she saw her sisters rising from the sea. They were as pale as she was, and their long beautiful hair no longer fluttered in the breeze. It had all been cut off.

"We traded our hair to the Sea Witch for her help, so that you wouldn't die!" they called out. "She's given us a knife. Here—see how keen the blade is? Before the sun rises, you must plunge it into the Prince's heart—and when his hot blood spatters your legs and feet, they'll grow together into a fishtail and you'll become a mermaid again! Then you can dive back down into the water and live out your three hundred years before turning into dead salty foam. Hurry! It's either him or you—one of you must die before the sun rises! Our old grandmother's grieving, so that her white hair all fell out, just as ours fell beneath the witch's scissors. Kill the Prince and come home! Quick, can't you see that red stripe in the sky? In a few minutes the sun will be up, and then you will die!" And with a strange deep sigh they sank back beneath the waves.

The little mermaid pulled back the purple curtain of the tent. She saw the beautiful bride sleeping with her head on the Prince's chest. She bowed down and kissed him on his lovely forehead, then glanced at the sky where the redness of dawn was spreading, and at the sharp knife in her hand. Then she fixed her eyes again upon the Prince. Dreaming, he spoke the name of his bride; all his thoughts were on her. The knife trembled as the mermaid held it—and then she flung it far into the waves. The sea flashed red where it fell, as if blood was oozing up from the water. She looked at him one last time, her eyes already glazing over, then plunged into the ocean and felt her body dissolve into foam.

The sun was rising from the sea. Its rays fell gentle and warm upon the deathly cold sea foam—but the little mermaid didn't *feel* dead. She saw the bright sun, and up above her floated a hundred beautiful transparent beings. Through these beings she could see the ship's white sails and the sky's red clouds, and their voices shaped a melody so unearthly that no human ear could hear it, just as no human eye could see their forms. They floated on the air without wings, lifted only by their own lightness. And then the little mermaid saw that she had a body just like theirs, rising higher and higher from the foam.

"Who are you? Who am I joining?" she wondered aloud, and her voice sounded like the others, so unearthly that no music of this world could ever come close to it.

"We're sylphs—the daughters of the air!" they replied. "A mermaid has no soul, it's true, and she'll never receive one unless she earns the love of a human being. Her eternal life depends on that strange power. The daughters of the air don't have immortal souls either—but we can create one through good deeds. We fly to hot countries, where the stifling air of disease kills people, and we cool the air with our fans. We spread the scent of flowers, we refresh and we heal. When we've done this good work for three hundred years, we're granted an immortal soul and can take part in humans' eternal happiness. Poor little mermaid! You've tried with all your heart to do the same thing we do, and your suffering and patience has raised you to our realm and made you a sylph. And now, by doing good deeds for three hundred years, you too can earn an immortal soul."

And the little mermaid raised her clear arms towards God's sun, and for the very first time she felt tears.

On board ship, the sounds of chatter and life returned, and she watched as the Prince and his beautiful bride began to look for her. They gazed wistfully at the sparkling foam, as if they knew she had plunged into the waves. Unseen, the little mermaid kissed the bride's forehead and smiled at the Prince, and then she flew up with the other sylphs on a rosy cloud that sailed through the air.

"In three hundred years, this is how we'll float into God's kingdom!"

"We might get there even before that," whispered one of the sylphs. "We glide invisibly into the houses of people with children. And every day that we find a good child, who makes her parents glad and deserves their love, God shortens our trial period. The children have no idea that we're floating through their rooms, but every time one of them makes us smile with joy, a year is subtracted from the three hundred. But if we see a child who's naughty and mean, it makes us cry with sadness—and each tear adds another day to our trial!"

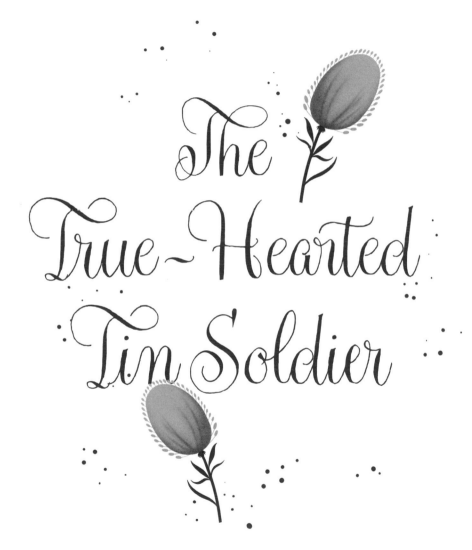

The
True~Hearted
Tin Soldier

NCE UPON A TIME there were twenty-five tin soldiers. They were brothers, because they were all sons of an old tin spoon. Each one held a rifle and looked straight in front of him, and their splendid uniforms were red and blue. The very first thing they ever heard was when the lid was lifted from the box where they lay. "Tin soldiers!" shouted a little boy, and he clapped his hands. They were a present for him because it was his birthday, and now he set them up on the table. Every soldier looked exactly like his brothers—except for one, who was a bit different. This soldier had only one leg, because he was the last to be cast and there hadn't been quite enough tin. Yet he stood just as steady on his one leg as the others on their two—and it's this soldier who would become something marvellous.

There were lots of other toys on the table where they were placed, but what caught the eye was an attractive paper castle. Through the tiny windows you could see right into its rooms. Outside the castle, little trees stood around a small mirror that was supposed to look like a lake, where wax swans swam in their own reflections. It all looked very pretty—but prettiest of all was the young dancer who stood in the middle of the castle's open doorway. She was also cut out of paper, but she was wearing a skirt of gauzy linen and a little blue sash across her shoulder, like a scarf. In the middle of the sash was a shiny spangle as big as her face. The dancer stretched out both arms, for she was a ballerina, and she raised one of her legs so high in the air that the tin soldier couldn't see it and thought she had only one leg—just like him.

That's the wife for me! he thought. *But she looks rather elegant, and lives in a castle, while I only have a box. And there are twenty-five of us living there—not a place for her! Yet I must try to introduce myself.* His tall body was hidden behind a snuffbox. Here he could gaze upon the fine little dancer, who kept standing on one leg without losing her balance.

Late in the evening, all the other tin soldiers were put into their box, and the people of the house went to bed. Now the toys started to play charades, fight battles and hold dances. The tin soldiers rattled in their box, because they wanted to get out but couldn't get the lid off. The nutcracker turned somersaults, the chalk played tricks on the slate, and they all made such a racket that it woke the canary, who began talking in rhyme. The only toys who didn't budge were the tin soldier and the ballerina. She stayed upright on tiptoe, with both her arms spread.

He was just as steady on his single leg, and his eyes didn't leave her for a moment.

Then the clock struck twelve and *smack!* the lid of the snuff box popped off. But there was no snuff tobacco inside, no, for up jumped a little black goblin—a jack-in-the-box!

"Tin soldier," warned the goblin, "keep your eyes to yourself."

But the tin soldier acted as if he hadn't heard.

"Well then," said the goblin, "just you wait till tomorrow!"

When morning came and the children got up, they placed the tin soldier on the windowsill. And it's not clear if it was because of the goblin or a gust of wind, but the window flew open—and the soldier tumbled head first from the third floor. He fell terribly fast, his leg in the air, and landed bang on his cap, his bayonet jammed between the cobblestones.

The young maid and the little boy rushed down to look for him immediately. But though they very nearly stepped on him, they didn't see him. If the tin soldier had shouted, "I'm here!" they probably would have found him, but he didn't think it proper to yell because he was in uniform.

Now it started raining, and each drop came quicker than the one before, until it was coming down in buckets. And when it stopped, two young mischief-makers came by.

"Ahoy!" the first boy called out. "A tin soldier! Time for him to join the navy."

Then they made a boat out of newspaper, put the tin soldier in it and sent him sailing down the gutter. The boys ran alongside, clapping their hands. My goodness! What waves there were in that gutter, and what a current—for remember, it had just rained buckets. The paper boat rocked up and down and spun around so quickly, the tin soldier started to shake. Yet he stayed standing and didn't blink, just looked straight ahead and held onto his rifle.

Suddenly the boat rushed into a long tunnel, where planks covered the gutter. It was just as dark in there as inside his box.

Where am I? he wondered. *This is the goblin's doing! If only the young dancer were sitting here in the boat, then I wouldn't mind if it were twice as dark!*

Just then there appeared a huge water rat, who lived in the gutter beneath the planks.

"Passport!" demanded the rat. "Hand it over!"

But the tin soldier said nothing; he just gripped his rifle even tighter. The boat kept moving with the rat right behind. Ooh, how it gnashed its teeth—and then it shouted to the floating sticks and straws, "Stop him, stop him! He hasn't paid the toll! He hasn't shown his passport!"

But the current started moving faster and faster, and now the tin soldier could see daylight where the planking ended. Yet he could also hear a roaring sound ahead of him that would scare the bravest of men, and soon he could see the gutter dropping away at the end of the tunnel, where the water fell into a large canal. It looked dangerous—as dangerous as the edge of a high waterfall would look to you!

But now it was so close that he couldn't stop. The boat shot out of the tunnel and the poor tin soldier held himself as stiff as a board—no one could say he moved a muscle. Then the boat splashed down, spun around three times and began to fill with water, up to the brim. It was sinking! Soon the tin soldier was standing in water up to his neck, and as the boat sank deeper and deeper, the newspaper started to come apart. As the water closed over the soldier's head, he thought of the delightful ballerina, whom he'd never see again. A children's song echoed in his ear:

Danger, danger, man of war—
You shall suffer death!

Then the paper split open and the tin soldier fell through the bottom—right into the mouth of an enormous fish!

Oh, but it was so dark inside! It was even worse than under the planks—and so cramped! But the tin soldier steeled himself, and he lay there in the fish as straight as a ramrod and gripped his rifle tight.

The fish swam every which way, and its movements squeezed the tin soldier dreadfully. After a long, long time it stopped moving and became quite still. . .

Then something flashed through it like a bolt of lightning. Bright light was everywhere, and someone shouted, "A tin soldier!" For the fish had been caught, sold in the market and brought up to a kitchen, where a young woman had sliced it open with a large knife. Now she grabbed the tin soldier by the waist with two fingers and carried him into a room, where everyone wanted to see the amazing man who had travelled in the belly of a fish.

Yet the tin soldier did not feel proud. They placed him up on a table, and there—oh, what strange things happen in this world! For the tin soldier found himself in the very same room as before. He saw the very same children and the very same toys on the table—including the pretty castle with the beautiful ballerina. She was still standing on one leg, with the other in the air, for she had stayed faithfully upright too. This touched the tin soldier, and he almost wept tin tears—but that would never do. He looked at her and she looked at him, and neither of them said a word.

Suddenly one of the small boys grabbed the tin soldier and threw him into the wood-burning stove. He didn't say why, but it must have been the goblin's fault.

The tin soldier stood inside the stove, all lit up, and he felt a terrible heat—but whether it came from fire or from love, he didn't know. His bright colours were all gone now, though no one could say if it was because of his long journey or simply because of his sorrow. He gazed at the young dancer and she gazed at him, and he felt that he was melting. Yet still he stood upright with his rifle in his hand. Then a door opened and the wind caught the dancer. She flew through the air like a sylph, straight to the tin soldier in the stove. She flared up in the fire and was gone. Then the tin soldier melted into a metal blob.

The next day, when the maid came to take out the ashes she found he'd become a small tin heart. But the only thing left of the ballerina was her spangle, and that was burnt black as coal.

PUSHKIN CHILDREN'S BOOKS

We created Pushkin Children's Books to share tales from different languages and cultures with younger readers, and to open the door to the wide, colourful worlds these stories offer.

From picture books and adventure stories to fairy tales and classics, and from fifty-year-old bestsellers to current huge successes abroad, the books on the Pushkin Children's list reflect the very best stories from around the world, for our most discerning readers of all: children.

THE BEGINNING WOODS
MALCOLM MCNEILL

'I loved every word and was envious of quite a few... A modern classic. Rich, funny and terrifying'
Eoin Colfer

THE RED ABBEY CHRONICLES
MARIA TURTSCHANINOFF

1 · *Maresi*
2 · *Naondel*

'Embued with myth, wonder, and told with a dazzling, compelling ferocity'
Kiran Millwood Hargrave, author of *The Girl of Ink and Stars*

THE LETTER FOR THE KING
TONKE DRAGT

'*The Letter for the King* will get pulses racing... Pushkin Press deserves every praise for publishing this beautifully translated, well-presented and captivating book'
The Times

THE SECRETS OF THE WILD WOOD
TONKE DRAGT

'Offers intrigue, action and escapism'
Sunday Times

THE SONG OF SEVEN
TONKE DRAGT

'A cracking adventure... so nail-biting you'll need to wear protective gloves'
The Times

THE MURDERER'S APE
JAKOB WEGELIUS

'A thrilling adventure. Prepare to meet the remarkable Sally Jones; you won't soon forget her'
Publishers Weekly

THE PARENT TRAP · THE FLYING CLASSROOM · DOT AND ANTON
ERICH KÄSTNER
Illustrated by Walter Trier

'The bold line drawings by Walter Trier are the work of genius... As for the stories, if you're a fan of *Emil and the Detectives*, then you'll find these just as spirited'
Spectator

FROM THE MIXED-UP FILES OF MRS. BASIL E. FRANKWEILER
E. L. KONIGSBURG

'Delightful... I love this book... a beautifully written adventure, with endearing characters and full of dry wit, imagination and inspirational confidence'
Daily Mail

THE RECKLESS SERIES
CORNELIA FUNKE
1 · *The Petrified Flesh*
2 · *Living Shadows*
3 · *The Golden Yarn*

'A wonderful storyteller'
Sunday Times

THE WILDWITCH SERIES
LENE KAABERBØL
1 · *Wildfire*
2 · *Oblivion*
3 · *Life Stealer*
4 · *Bloodling*

'Classic fantasy adventure... Young readers will be delighted to hear that there are more adventures to come for Clara'
Lovereading

MEET AT THE ARK AT EIGHT!
ULRICH HUB
Illustrated by Jörg Mühle

'Of all the books about a penguin in a suitcase pretending to be God asking for a cheesecake, this one is absolutely, definitely my favourite'
Independent

THE SNOW QUEEN
HANS CHRISTIAN ANDERSEN
Illustrated by Lucie Arnoux

'A lovely edition [of a] timeless story'
The Lady

THE WILD SWANS
HANS CHRISTIAN ANDERSEN

'A fresh new translation of these two classic fairy tales recreates the
lyrical beauty and pathos of the Danish genius' evergreen stories'
The Bay

THE CAT WHO CAME IN OFF THE ROOF
ANNIE M.G. SCHMIDT

'Guaranteed to make anyone 7-plus to 107 who likes to
curl up with a book and a cat purr with pleasure'
The Times

LAFCADIO: THE LION WHO SHOT BACK
SHEL SILVERSTEIN

'A story which is really funny, yet also teaches us a great
deal about what we want, what we think we want and what
we are no longer certain about once we have it'
Irish Times

THE SECRET OF THE BLUE GLASS
TOMIKO INUI

'I love this book... How important it is, in these times, that our children
read the stories from other peoples, other cultures, other times'
Michael Morpurgo, *Guardian*

THE STORY OF THE BLUE PLANET
ANDRI SNÆR MAGNASON
Illustrated by Áslaug Jónsdóttir

'A Seussian mix of wonder, wit and gravitas'
The New York Times

THE WITCH IN THE BROOM CUPBOARD AND OTHER TALES

PIERRE GRIPARI

Illustrated by Fernando Puig Rosado

'Wonderful... funny, tender and daft'

David Almond

CLEMENTINE LOVES RED

KRYSTYNA BOGLAR

'A dizzying dance'

Ricochet Jeunes

SHOLA AND THE LIONS

BERNARDO ATXAGA

Illustrated by Mikel Valverde

'Gently ironic stories... totally charming'

Independent

PIGLETTES

CLEMENTINE BEAUVAIS

'A jubilant novel that will make you smile. A true joy'

Le Monde

SAVE THE STORY

GULLIVER · ANTIGONE · CAPTAIN NEMO · DON JUAN
GILGAMESH · THE BETROTHED · THE NOSE
CYRANO DE BERGERAC · KING LEAR · CRIME AND PUNISHMENT

'An amazing new series from Pushkin Press in which literary, adult authors
retell classics (with terrific illustrations) for a younger generation'

Daily Telegraph

THE OKSA POLLOCK SERIES

ANNE PLICHOTA AND CENDRINE WOLF

1 · *The Last Hope*
2 · *The Forest of Lost Souls*
3 · *The Heart of Two Worlds*
4 · *Tainted Bonds*

'A feisty heroine, lots of sparky tricks and evil opponents could
fill a gap left by the end of the Harry Potter series'

Daily Mail